Princess Power

The Perfectly Proper Prince

By Suzanne Williams

Illustrated by Chuck Gonzales

HarperTrophy®
An Imprint of HarperCollins*Publishers*

The Perfectly Proper Prince
 For information address HarperCollins Children's Books, a division of HarperCollins Publishers, 1350 Avenue of the Americas, New York, NY 10019.
www.harpercollinschildrens.com

Library of Congress Cataloging-in-Publication Data is available.
ISBN-10: 0-06-078299-4 (trade) — ISBN-13: 978-0-06-078299-3 (trade)
ISBN-10: 0-06-078298-6 (pbk.) — ISBN-13: 978-0-06-078298-6 (pbk.)

Typography by Jennifer Bankenstein
❖
First Harper Trophy edition, 2006

To Mark, my perfectly
lovable prince

Contents

Princess Lysandra

"OUCH!" PRINCESS LYSANDRA THREW DOWN her embroidery and sucked at her finger. "I hate sewing!" she said crossly. "My needle is always pricking me."

Princess Gabriella, Lysandra's older sister, looked up from her own stitching and frowned. "Practice makes perfect."

"But sewing's not something I *want* to be perfect at," Lysandra grumbled. "Why can't I learn to use a sword, like Cousin Owen?" Her cousin had begun fencing lessons a year ago when he turned ten, the same age Lysandra was now.

Brushing back her golden locks, Gabriella sighed. "You know the reason. Princesses have no need for swords."

"And no need for husbands either, right?" Lysandra said, slyly changing the subject.

Gabriella blushed. "That's not true. I'd marry

in a minute if the right prince came along."

"What was wrong with the last one?"

"Prince Hubert?" Gabriella sniffed. "He had the table manners of a pig. He rooted around in his food and mixed his peas with his mashed potatoes. He chewed with his mouth open and picked his teeth with his knife."

"So what's wrong with that?" Most of the men in the kingdom chewed with their mouths open and picked their teeth with their knives. And as for mixing peas in mashed potatoes, Lysandra thought they tasted better that way.

"'Good manners reveal a fine mind; bad manners, a poor one,'" recited Gabriella.

That saying, Lysandra knew, came from Gabriella's favorite book: *Courtly Manners and Duties.* Gabriella had studied the book so much the binding was falling apart.

Lysandra picked up her sewing again.

"What about Prince Lowell?" It had been three years since he'd visited the castle, but Lysandra still remembered his elegant mustache.

"*His* table manners were perfect," Gabriella said with a sigh, "but he sang like a crow and couldn't dance three steps without tripping over his feet or, worse, mine."

Lysandra struggled to untangle her thread. She could live without dancing if she could learn to use a sword. Gabriella was just too picky. She'd come close to marrying once, but that was years ago, when Lysandra was only a baby. Though she wondered what had happened to break off that engagement, she never asked. Gabriella was touchy about her love life. It seemed *no* man would ever be perfect enough to suit her. And at twenty-five she was almost too old to wed; most princesses were married by the age of sixteen.

Lysandra stabbed at her embroidery, piercing

her finger again. "A plague upon this needle!" she yelled.

Gabriella lifted a perfectly shaped eyebrow. "Princesses do not swear."

Lysandra pressed her lips together to keep from saying worse. Once she'd read about a princess who pricked her finger on a spindle and fell asleep for a hundred years. That didn't sound so bad—especially if it meant a hundred years without sewing.

To Lysandra's relief, the trumpets blew, announcing the beginning of the midday rest period. With a small yawn, Gabriella set down her embroidery and rose from her red velvet chair. "Come along," she said to Lysandra. "Time for our naps."

After leaving the Sewing Chamber, the two princesses made their way down a short corridor to the bedchamber they shared. Lysandra would've preferred a separate room, but Gabriella liked having company. That's what she said, anyway. What Gabriella *really* liked, Lysandra suspected, was having someone around to nag. Nevertheless, to spare Gabriella's feelings, Lysandra kept on rooming with her.

When they reached their room, a chambermaid was waiting to help the two princesses out of their gowns. Before climbing into bed, Lysandra checked to make sure the magic purse she always wore around her neck was still there. A gift from her father, King Sheldon II, the purse refilled with gold coins whenever it was empty. Though Lysandra was careful to keep the purse safe, anybody stealing it would get a nasty surprise. When it was opened by anyone except Lysandra, swarms of bees flew out and pursued the thief.

Truthfully, however, Lysandra never had much use for her purse. Most of the things she was allowed to spend money on—gowns and sweets, for example—weren't things she cared all that much about. Well, she enjoyed sweets, but she could only eat so many of them before she made herself sick . . . or got a toothache.

But there was *one* thing she enjoyed spending her coins on. Lysandra glanced across the room toward Gabriella. Her soft snores signaled that she was asleep. *Good.*

Reaching under her pillow, Lysandra pulled out a book. It had been worth all the gold coins she'd spent on it. An adventure story, the book was about a prince who was on a quest to find a magical herb to cure his sick father. Along the way the prince battled an ogre with eight heads, slew three dragons, and outwitted an evil sorcerer.

Lysandra wished *she* could have adventures like that. It was frustrating to only be able to read about them. And even that had to be done in secret. Princesses weren't supposed to read adventure stories—just poetry and romances, and the etiquette books that Gabriella favored.

After she finished her chapter, Lysandra closed her book and hid it under her pillow

again. She threw off her sheets and slipped out of bed. Then she wrapped herself in a brown woolen cloak, pulling up the hood to hide her wavy blond hair. Then, tiptoeing so as not to wake Gabriella, Lysandra escaped their room.

The Sword Fight

LYSANDRA CREPT TO THE END OF THE CORRIDOR, then ran downstairs to a small room that overlooked the castle courtyard. The thud of wooden swords on wooden shields met her ears. Below, Lysandra's cousin Owen and his friends, George and Henry, practiced fighting. Unlike princesses, boys didn't have to take naps. It was unfair. But Gabriella always said, "Princesses need their beauty sleep."

"Ow!" yelled Owen.

"I got you!" George pointed the tip of his wooden sword under Owen's large chin. "Now *I'm* the knight and *you* have to be my horse."

"No fair!" cried Owen. "My shield's too small. With a bigger one, you couldn't have gotten me."

Lysandra grinned. Owen always had some excuse for his poor fighting skills. In truth, his shield was slightly larger than the other boys' shields.

"Face it, Owen," said Henry. "George got you fair and square." Lysandra rather liked Henry. He was kind, and besides, he could squirt a fine stream of water between his two front teeth.

Owen's face went red. "That's it! I'm through playing with the two of you!" Tossing his sword and shield, he ran off.

George and Henry looked at each other

and shrugged. Then they raised their swords and shields and went on with their game, charging each other and slashing the air between them.

Pretending she held a sword and shield too, Lysandra copied their moves, adding some fancy footwork. *Take that, Troll!* she thought as she swung her imaginary sword. Not that she'd ever seen a troll, of course. The rare times she was allowed outside the castle, she had only caught a glimpse of the

countryside as it passed in front of her carriage.

Lysandra rested her imaginary sword in the middle of the imaginary troll's massive chest. "I will let you go," she said, "if you leave the kingdom and never come back."

"R-R-R-R-ROAR!" came a growl from behind her.

Startled, Lysandra spun around so fast, her hood flew off.

"Got you!" Owen laughed. "I don't know

what you think you're playing at," he said. "Fighting is *man's* work. Why, even the smallest troll could swallow you in a single gulp."

Lysandra drew herself up. "Not if I could defend myself."

"Don't be ridiculous," Owen said, sneering. "You're a *princess*, remember? Sneaking out during your nap, pretending to fight trolls. . . ." He shook his head. "I can't *wait* to tell your mother."

Lysandra looked at him in alarm. "Please don't tell." She plucked nervously at the purse strap around her neck.

"Please don't tell," Owen mimicked in a high voice. Then he grinned. "Tell you what. Give me enough coins for a *real* sword and shield, and I'll forget I saw you—this time."

Sighing, Lysandra opened her purse and shook a large pile of coins into Owen's outstretched hand. She knew her uncle, Owen's father, would never allow Owen to buy a *real* sword and shield. Owen would likely spend the money on sweets instead. She hoped he'd end up with a horrible stomachache.

"Thanks," Owen grunted, pocketing the coins. "Now scoot," he said, "or I might change my mind."

Lysandra fled back to her room. Gabriella was still napping. Thinking hateful thoughts about Owen, Lysandra flung off her cloak and crawled into bed. Without meaning to, she fell asleep. She dreamed she was battling an enormous troll that had eaten several villagers. The handle of her silver sword gleamed with diamonds, emeralds, and rubies. "Take that, you beast!" Lysandra struck out with her sword. It flashed within an inch of the troll's hairy hide.

The troll reared back, his tiny eyes flickering with fear. Compared to the size of his body, his head was quite small. But he had a large chin—curiously like her cousin Owen's. In fact, the troll looked a lot like Owen. Besides the chin, he had the same beady eyes and sneer.

Lysandra pointed her sword at the troll's chest. "I've got you now!" she exclaimed.

"No fair," whined the troll. "If I were bigger, you couldn't have gotten me."

"What?" Lysandra couldn't believe his nonsense. The troll was taller than the castle's highest tower and as big around as the moat. "I got you fair and square," she said. "Now leave."

"Fine," said the troll, pouting. "I don't want to stay here anyway!"

As it stomped off, Lysandra felt a stab of pity for the troll. He might be an enormous, human-eating bully, but at heart he was nothing but a big baby. She opened her purse and flung several handfuls of gold after him. "Buy yourself a cartload of meat pies!" she shouted.

Gabriella's voice interrupted Lysandra's dream. "Wake up, Sleepyhead. It's time to redecorate the Crystal Ball Room."

Lysandra groaned. Next to sewing, decorating was her least favorite thing to do, and the Crystal Ball Room had to be constantly redone. Not a place for dances, as some people might think, the Crystal Ball Room was where her mother kept their crystal ball. It was the cleanest room in the castle, dusted by chambermaids five times a day. Fresh-cut flowers, replaced daily, stood on highly polished tabletops. And even though the room was rarely used, a fire roared in the fireplace all day and all night.

The reason for this care was simple: If anyone looked in on them from a crystal ball in another castle or palace, this was the room they would see. And her family's castle *had* to be seen in the best possible light. But, really, it was rather silly. Everyone knew Crystal Ball Rooms were only for show. Even the shabbiest castles had nice-looking Crystal Ball Rooms.

"Since you're just now getting up," said Gabriella, "I'll go on ahead. Meet me there in a few minutes, all right?"

Lysandra nodded, but she took her time getting dressed. When she finally entered the Crystal Ball Room, two workmen were already busily repainting the wall, changing the color from midnight blue to dusky pink. A chambermaid was arranging red roses in a crystal vase, and Gabriella was pinning up some of new curtains. She spotted Lysandra. "Find something to cover up the crystal ball, will you, please?" No one was supposed to see the room before the changes were complete.

Feeling bored already, Lysandra found a

cloth and placed it over the ball. Surely there must be other princesses like herself—others she hadn't yet met—who longed for a more adventurous life. If only there was a way to find them.

Lysandra stared at the covered crystal ball, and slowly an idea came to her. It was such a great idea, she didn't know why she hadn't thought of it before.

Calling All Princesses

"MAY I BE EXCUSED FOR A FEW MINUTES?" Lysandra asked Gabriella.

Gabriella frowned. "But you only just got here."

"Please? I'll only be gone a little while."

"Well, all right," Gabriella said with a sigh.

"Thanks." Lysandra ran down the corridor to her mother's chamber. Queen Rowena was in her sitting room, reading a book of poetry.

Her auburn hair flowed long and shiny over the shoulders of her light green gown.

"May I place a sign in front of the crystal ball?" Lysandra asked breathlessly.

Her mother closed her book. "What kind of a sign, dear?"

"A sign announcing a talent show," Lysandra said, crossing her fingers behind her back. Truthfully, she wasn't interested in putting on a show. It was the *auditions* she was after. She hoped they would help her find others like herself—and perhaps even help her uncover some princesses with talents that could be useful during an adventure.

"What an interesting idea," said her mother. "And who would you invite?"

"Princesses around my age," Lysandra said.

Queen Rowena smiled. "Sounds like fun, but maybe you'd better ask your father. Make sure it's okay with him."

"All right." Dropping a quick curtsy, Lysandra left in search of her father. After running up and down several corridors, she finally found him having a snack in his library. King Sheldon II had pastry crumbs in his beard, but Lysandra didn't mention it.

He smiled at her. "How's my favorite younger daughter?"

Lysandra grinned. "I'm your *only* younger daughter, and I'm fine." Then she explained about her talent show idea. "So is it all right with you?" she asked when she'd finished.

The king wrinkled his brow. "Sounds to me like something you should ask your mother."

Lysandra sighed. You'd think a king or queen would be good at making decisions. Yet her parents could never seem to give her a straight answer when she needed one. "If it's okay with you, it's okay with her," she said.

"If it's okay with her, it's okay with me," the king replied.

Lysandra decided to take that as a "yes."

She raced back to the Crystal Ball Room and told Gabriella the good news about the talent show.

"It's nice to see you taking an interest in an activity befitting a princess," said Gabriella. "I'll help paint the sign if you'd like. And I can judge the auditions, too."

Lysandra gulped. "Thank you." She welcomed the help on the sign; Gabriella's handwriting was far better than Lysandra's. Yet Gabriella's idea of "talent" was probably miles apart from her own.

When the sign was ready, Lysandra propped it in front of the crystal ball. Anyone peering in from another castle or palace would see the sign right away. It read:

A TALENT SHOW!
***
King Sheldon II's Castle, Kingdom of Zamora
Auditions: June 20th
Show: June 24th
For all interested princesses ages 8-13
***
PRIZES!* FUN! FRIENDSHIP!
*For the top ten acts
***
R.S.V.P. to Princess Lysandra
by June 10th.

"I do hope we get a good turnout," said Gabriella.

"So do I," said Lysandra.

By June tenth, thirty-three princesses had RSVPed. The castle was a hive of activity as servants buzzed from one room to another preparing additional sleeping chambers, washing linens, finding extra dishes, and cooking lots of food.

"We're going to need a stage," Gabriella said. "I'll get some workmen on it right away."

"Can't we just use the Audience Room and string up a curtain?" asked Lysandra.

Gabriella's eyes widened in horror. "Of course not! The Audience Room might be suitable for auditions, but we'll want to invite lots and lots of people to the show."

Lysandra gulped. If things went the way she hoped, there might not be an actual show. But she could hardly tell Gabriella that.

Before long the sound of hammers, axes, saws, and chisels filled the air as the castle carpenters began construction of a huge wooden stage in the courtyard. The royal gardeners planted rows and rows of rosebushes on both sides.

"Where are we supposed to fight?" Owen complained to Lysandra.

Henry, who was drinking from a silver goblet, spit a long stream of cider between his teeth. "How about down by the stables?"

"Sounds good to me," said George.

As the boys walked away, Owen cast Lysandra a nasty look.

Finally, on the afternoon before the auditions, the princesses began to arrive. From a tower room overlooking the castle walls, Lysandra watched the first few horse-drawn carriages rumble over the drawbridge. She raced down to the Great Hall to join Gabriella and Queen Rowena in receiving the princesses.

At first they seemed a very ordinary lot: beautiful and well-mannered, of course, but not terribly exciting. But as the ninth princess stepped forward to curtsy, Lysandra felt a strong rush of wind enter the Hall. Looking up, Lysandra saw a girl on a flying carpet. The carpet zoomed from the ceiling to the floor and came to an abrupt halt at Lysandra's feet.

The princess riding the carpet tumbled off. "Whoa there. Sorry!" she cried, jumping up. Then she swayed, as if she might faint.

"Are you okay?" asked Lysandra.

The girl grinned. "I'm fine. Just dizzy." She curtsied clumsily. "Princess Fatima. Glad to meet you."

Lysandra studied Princess Fatima as Queen Rowena spoke with her. She had long black hair, dark skin, and almond-shaped eyes. She was wearing a pink silk blouse and purple pantaloons that resembled a skirt split into trousers. Her feet were bare.

Gabriella rang a little bell and a chambermaid came into the Hall. "Please take Princess Fatima to her quarters. I'm sure she'd like to change into more *proper* attire."

Princess Fatima blushed. "But this is how I always dress. I don't even own a skirt. It would just fly up when I travel."

Gabriella sniffed. "I'm sure we can find you a suitable gown among Lysandra's things. You seem to be about her size."

"I think you look fine just as you are," said Lysandra. Gabriella was so rude! "But if you *want* to borrow something of mine, you can."

"Thank you," said Princess Fatima. "But I'd rather stay as I am." She curtsied again, then went off to sit with the other princesses.

Lysandra watched her walk away. Maybe if she apologized to Fatima later on for Gabriella's remark, Fatima would offer to give her a ride on the flying carpet. With a flying carpet, one could go anywhere! Fatima seemed like just the kind of princess Lysandra had been wishing to meet. She hoped there'd be others like her at the auditions tomorrow.

The Auditions

Lysandra checked her list of names. "Princess Penelope!" she called out. It was the seventh name on her list. The first six princesses to audition that morning had included two singers and four dancers. The first singer had been dreadful, but the second was pretty good, though she'd had to stretch her voice to reach the high notes. The dancers could waltz and twirl wonderfully, but that wasn't the kind of talent Lysandra was after. What use would singing and dancing be during an adventure?

A red velvet curtain had been installed in the Audience Room for the auditions. It parted now and Princess Penelope walked out, holding a golden ball.

Gabriella leaned forward in her chair. "Please tell us your talent."

Princess Penelope, short and stout, smiled dreamily. "I'm a juggler."

"Where are your other balls?" asked Gabriella, frowning.

"Other balls?" Penelope looked confused. "I only juggle *one*." She threw her golden ball a foot in the air and caught it. Then she threw it a little higher and caught it again. After five or six times, Gabriella stopped her.

"I think I might be able to throw a little

higher still," said Penelope. "Want me to try?"

Gabriella pursed her lips. "No, thank you. That's quite enough."

The next several princesses were also a pretty worthless lot. One princess held up a "magic" seashell. In a mysterious voice she said, "If you hold this to your ear, you'll hear the ocean."

"What a nitwit," Lysandra muttered under her breath. "Everyone knows that old trick."

Next Princess Minerva took off her shoes and showed the girls that her second toes were longer than her big toes. She was followed by a princess with *webbed* toes who released a jar of flies, then flicked an amazingly long tongue out of her mouth and zapped the flies up one by one. It seemed like a pretty

good trick until another princess exposed her as a witch's mistake—a frog turned into a princess.

Hiding a smile, Lysandra consulted her list. "Princess Elena," she called out.

Princess Elena was slim and graceful,

with soft, hazel eyes and frizzy brown hair. She recited a poem about a mermaid and a sea serpent. Elena had a lovely, soothing voice and recited well, but Lysandra didn't think she seemed the adventurous type.

"Very nice," Gabriella said, nodding appreciatively when Elena had finished.

Elena blinked as if unaware that anyone

had been listening. "Thank you." She curtsied shyly, then sat down to watch the rest of the auditions.

"Princess Tansy!" Lysandra called out when there were only five princesses left to perform.

The curtains parted and out stepped a boyish-looking girl with short, ginger-colored hair and freckles. She held up a wooden instrument. "This is a magic flute," she said.

Gabriella rolled her eyes. "And what's magic about it?" she asked wearily.

"It was carved by a wizard and sings what people are thinking."

"O-*kay*," Gabriella said, plainly disbelieving.

Tansy pressed her lips to the flute and began to play. A sprightly melody floated through the air and made Lysandra feel like dancing. Suddenly a swirl of voices rose above the melody. Lysandra was startled to hear the thought she'd had just a moment ago come

drifting back to her: *This music makes me feel like dancing.*

Then she heard one of Gabriella's thoughts: *That's not a proper flute. A proper flute is shiny and silver with sweeter-sounding tones.*

She plays prettily enough, but what a horrible

haircut, came a thought from a princess who had already auditioned. *And that dress she's wearing hangs on her like a flour sack.*

I wish I hadn't muffed my last cartwheel, came another thought. *What if I don't make it into the talent show?*

Finally the song came to an end. Grinning mischievously, Tansy pulled her flute away from her lips. "Just so everyone knows," she said, "this *is* a proper flute, I *like* my haircut, and this happens to be my *favorite* dress." She gave a bow instead of a curtsy, then disappeared behind the curtain.

Gabriella's jaw dropped. "Well, I never!"

Lysandra smiled. She was going to have to get to know Tansy better.

Of the next three princesses, the first could wiggle her ears, the second could fold herself into a pretzel, and the third could cross her eyes, whistle, and tap-dance all at the same time. The very last princess to audition was Princess Fatima. She glided through the curtain on her flying carpet and performed a dizzying variety of loop the loops, figure eights, and sudden drops from the ceiling. It was during one of these drops that she lost her hold and tumbled head over heels onto the floor, badly skinning one knee.

"Bats and bullfrogs!" she exclaimed loudly.

Seeming more horrified at Princess Fatima's outburst than her injury, most of the princesses covered their ears. But Princess Elena rushed to Fatima's side. Swiftly Elena pulled a small blue bottle from the folds of her gown. She poured several drops of a white, creamy lotion into her hand, then gently applied the lotion to Fatima's knee, which healed instantly.

Now *that* was a useful talent, thought Lysandra. Maybe she'd misjudged the shy, poetry-reading princess after all.

Fatima stood up. After testing her knee with a few practice kicks, she hugged Elena. "Thanks! You're terrific."

Lysandra nodded. *Fatima, Tansy, and Elena.* Those would be *her* top choices for talent—and, she hoped, for future friends.

The Departures

"I'VE COMPILED A LIST OF THE TOP TEN ACTS," Gabriella said to Lysandra after the other princesses had left to prepare for dinner.

Lysandra scanned Gabriella's list. Of the three princesses whom Lysandra had chosen, Gabriella had only picked Elena. "Well, at least we agree on her," Lysandra said, pointing to Elena's name.

Gabriella nodded. "She recites very well,

doesn't she? And did you know she asked to borrow my copy of *Courtly Manners and Duties* when she saw me reading it last night? Of course I gave it to her right away."

"Hmm," said Lysandra. In her mind, wanting to read *Courtly Manners and Duties* was a black mark against Elena. But she still approved of Elena's healing abilities and her kindness to Fatima. "Why aren't Princess Fatima and Princess Tansy on your list?" she asked. "I thought they had the best acts of all."

Gabriella sniffed. "I don't think riding a flying carpet should be classified as a 'talent,' since the carpet does all the work. Besides, Princess Fatima fell off. As for Princess Tansy, her technique was good, but some of her notes were flat. And I am firmly of the opinion that one's thoughts should remain private."

Lysandra frowned. "But Tansy and Fatima

are *my* choices. Please add them to your list."

"But we said we'd only pick *ten*," Gabriella protested. "It wouldn't be proper to choose twelve."

Lysandra crossed her arms stubbornly. "Then take two off *your* list."

"I can't do that," Gabriella said, just as stubbornly as Lysandra.

In the end, however, Gabriella reluctantly agreed to twelve acts. Lysandra announced the finalists in the Banquet Hall during dinner. There were applause for the winners and groans and a few tears from the losers. The next morning the twenty-one princesses who hadn't been chosen departed the castle.

Now that the auditions were over, Lysandra was eager to spend time with the three princesses she wanted to befriend. She couldn't have cared less about the talent show.

After sending for Fatima, Tansy, and Elena, Lysandra asked them to wait for her in her bedchamber. She wasn't worried about Gabriella coming up to their room, as she and Queen Rowena had gone for a walk in the Royal Gardens. The three princesses looked at Lysandra questioningly but did as she asked.

Meanwhile, Lysandra snuck into her mother's room. She painted her face and neck with bright red spots and drew dark lines under her eyes. Then she gathered the remaining nine princesses together. In the most pathetic voice she could manage, Lysandra said, "I'm very sorry to have to tell you this, but last night I came down with the plague." She coughed without covering her mouth. The nine princesses squealed and scooted as far away from her as they could get.

Lysandra faked a sneeze. "I'm afraid the talent show will have to be cancelled," she said in a croaky voice, "but I promised prizes, so . . . " Pulling her magic purse from around her neck, she poured a pile of coins onto a table. "You may each help yourself to fifty coins. Just think of all the new gowns and miles of embroidery thread you'll be able to buy!"

When the nine princesses hesitated to pick up the coins, Lysandra said, "Don't worry. They're plague-free. I haven't even touched them."

Sighing with relief, the princesses scrambled to pick up the coins. "Please don't mention my illness to anyone," Lysandra said, "especially not to Gabriella. She doesn't know I'm sick, and the doctor says she's likely to get it too. I don't want her to know until she must." She paused and coughed again. "Even though Gabriella isn't showing symptoms yet, she's probably highly contagious. You might want to skip saying good-bye to her when you leave."

With coins clutched in their fists, the nine

ITCH
ITCH

princesses edged around Lysandra, keeping as far away from her as possible. Once the princesses were out of the room, they raced down the corridors to their quarters, packed up their belongings, and fled. Lysandra couldn't help grinning as the drawbridge was lowered and nine horse-drawn carriages thundered across and into the countryside.

Lysandra Explains

LYSANDRA PULLED OUT A LACE HANDKERCHIEF and wiped off her makeup, then ran to her bedchamber. Fatima, Tansy, and Elena looked up as she burst into the room. A frown played at the corners of Fatima's mouth. "We've been waiting here for over an hour—"

"Sorry," Lysandra said quickly. "It couldn't be helped."

"What's up?" asked Tansy, who was

polishing her flute with a rag.

Lysandra looked at the princesses. "I'm afraid there won't be any talent show after all."

Elena's soft, hazel eyes widened. "Why not?"

Hoping they wouldn't hate her for what she'd done, Lysandra took a deep breath. "Because I sent all the others away."

"What?" exclaimed Fatima. "Are you nuts?"

Tansy just looked amused. Maybe she didn't care all that much about the talent show, anyway.

Laying a hand on Fatima's arm, Elena said, "Let's hear what Lysandra has to say."

Lysandra plopped down beside them. "I wanted to meet other princesses my age," she explained. "The auditions were a way to do that. Now there's no need for a talent show."

Fatima's dark eyes flashed. "Why, of all the cheap tricks—"

Lysandra held up a hand. "No, wait. You

have to understand. I hate sewing, and dressing up, and doing all the other things a proper princess does. I want *adventure*."

"Well, what's that got to do with us?" Fatima asked, sounding more puzzled than angry now.

"I picked the three of you because . . . well, because you were different from the others," Lysandra explained. "You seemed like fun. I thought maybe the four of us could have adventures together."

The three princesses looked at her in surprise. "What are you getting at?" asked Tansy. "You want the four of us to form some kind of a . . . *club*?"

Lysandra nodded. "Only in *our* club we'd do exciting things—like rescuing townspeople from a fire-breathing dragon."

Fatima cocked her head. "That would be exciting all right."

"Maybe *too* exciting," said Elena.

Lysandra grinned. "Well, we could start with a smaller, easier adventure."

"Like what?" Elena asked.

"I don't know. But we could search for one."

Fatima nodded. "I'm beginning to like your idea."

"You can count me in," said Tansy.

"Me too," said Elena.

Footsteps sounded in the corridor. "Shh," Lysandra said hurriedly. "It's probably Gabriella. She doesn't know I cancelled the talent show yet."

Sure enough, Gabriella strode into the room. "The oddest thing just happened—," she said, then stopped when she noticed the three princesses with Lysandra. "Pardon me. I didn't see you had company."

"It's okay," said Lysandra. "Go on."

Gabriella sank onto a cushion. "I was out

in the courtyard overseeing the final work on the stage when Princess Lavinia, one of the dancers, came running by. I called to her and she shrieked as if I was some kind of monster! Then she covered her mouth with her handkerchief and raced away like the devil was after her."

Fatima looked at Lysandra and lifted an eyebrow.

Lysandra pretended not to notice. "How very strange," she said. "Listen, Gabriella, I'm sorry to have to tell you this, but nine of the twelve princesses who were supposed to perform in the talent show, including Princess Lavinia, have gone home."

"What?" Gabriella's face went pale. "Why would they do that?"

Tansy piped up. "Stage fright?"

Gabriella shook her head. "What are we supposed to do now?"

"You've still got the three of us," Elena said with a smile.

Gabriella looked at them suspiciously. "So why are the three of you the only ones who stayed?"

"Because Lysandra asked us to," said Fatima

matter-of-factly. "Besides," she said, looking around at the others, "we don't suffer from stage fright." She smiled at Gabriella. "Would you still like us to perform?"

"Three acts wouldn't be nearly enough," said Gabriella.

But Lysandra knew—and felt sure Fatima did, too—that Gabriella hadn't cared much for the flying-carpet act. Nor had she liked having her thoughts revealed by Tansy's magic flute.

"Why don't we call back some of the others?" Lysandra suggested slyly. "I bet we could get Princess Penelope and her one-ball juggling act."

"Or the Magic Seashell Princess," Elena added.

Tansy grinned. "I liked Princess Minerva with the long second toes."

Gabriella groaned. "It's no good. We'll have to cancel the show." She rose to her feet, mumbling "very improper business, indeed" and "things like this just aren't done" as she went out the door.

Fatima turned to Lysandra. "About those nine princesses . . . why did they *really* leave?"

Lysandra blushed. "I told them I had the plague. It was the only thing I could think of that would get them to leave quickly."

Fatima and Tansy laughed so hard that tears rolled down their faces.

Elena shook her head, but Lysandra could see she was smiling.

Up and Away

THAT NIGHT GABRIELLA SLEPT IN ANOTHER room so that the princesses could share the bedchamber with Lysandra. The four girls talked and giggled late into the night. Lysandra had never had so much fun.

Tansy, who at nine was the youngest of the princesses, had *six* brothers. "All of them are big practical jokers," she said. "They'd make my life miserable if it wasn't for my flute. It's the only way I can find out ahead of time when they're scheming to put snakes in my bed or worms in my porridge."

Elena, on the other hand, was eleven and an only child. She loved books and had an amazing ability to remember whatever she read. It was part of the reason she was so good at reciting poetry. To Lysandra's relief, Elena didn't think much of *Courtly Manners and Duties.* "'The refined lady prefers polite conversation and sewing to reading,'" she recited. "'Too much reading tires the brain.' What rubbish. The only reading that tires my brain is this book!"

"It's perfect nonsense," Fatima agreed. At twelve, she was the oldest of the four girls. Like Lysandra, she had one older sister. But her sister was married and had a baby, so Fatima was an aunt. She wrinkled her nose. "Speaking of nonsense, I don't know why everyone says babies are so adorable. My nephew, Hassim, smells funny, and his bald head looks like a squashed pumpkin!"

Before the princesses went to sleep, they vowed to search for an adventure the very next day, hoping to find someone in need of their help. "We can wait until the midday rest period," said Lysandra, "then sneak out of the castle."

"How will we get out?" asked Tansy.

"We can use my flying carpet," said Fatima. "It's big enough for us all."

"Where shall we go?" Elena asked.

"How about the village?" suggested Lysandra. "There'll be lots of people at the market. Surely one of them will need our help."

And so it was settled. The next day, when the trumpets announced the rest period, the four princesses prepared for their adventure.

They were just about to climb onto Fatima's flying carpet when there was a knock at the door.

"Hide!" Lysandra whispered. Fatima, Elena, and Tansy dived onto the beds and pulled the covers over their heads as Lysandra crossed the room to open the door.

Gabriella glanced around the room suspiciously. "Just checking to make sure you were all tucked in," she said. "I heard you talking late last night and expect you didn't get much sleep. You know that's not good for princesses."

Lysandra rolled her eyes. " 'To be at your best, get plenty of rest,' " she recited in a singsong voice. A loud snore came from one of the beds, followed by muffled laughter.

Gabriella lifted a perfectly shaped eyebrow, but all she said was "Have a good nap." Turning on her heel, she left the room.

As soon as Gabriella's footsteps had faded away, Lysandra and her three new friends threw on old cloaks, then raced to the carpet. Following Fatima's example, Lysandra sat cross-legged behind her, while Tansy and Elena climbed on too. Fatima grasped the front edge of the carpet and it rose into the air.

"How do we keep from falling off?" Elena asked, sounding worried.

"Easy," said Fatima. "Just sit tight. I'll make sure it's a smooth ride. But if it'll make you

feel better, you can hold onto the side of the carpet."

The princesses sailed out of the bedchamber window and over the valley. A delicious thrill ran through Lysandra as they soared through the air with the wind rushing past their ears.

Grasping the side of the carpet with one hand and holding onto Fatima with the other, Lysandra looked down. The fields that surrounded the village below were a hodge-

podge of patchwork squares set off from one another by bright green hedges. Curling like a ribbon, a river ran through the center of town. Clustered near it, along a dusty road, were cottages and shops.

Fatima landed the carpet in an open meadow several blocks from the village square. After everyone climbed off, she rolled up the carpet tightly and strapped it onto her back. Lysandra hoped no one had spotted them as they were flying. It wouldn't be good to have news of their adventure getting back to the castle . . . especially if the news reached Gabriella or her parents!

Following the ringing of church bells and the clanking of blacksmiths' hammers, the princesses walked toward the middle of town. As they neared the market in the village square, they heard hawkers selling their wares, children shouting, and babies bawling. A cart wheel squealed, and the princesses scrambled out of the way as a peddler's wagon lurched past.

Lysandra had only viewed the market from the inside of a carriage before. Now, with the other princesses at her heels, she rushed delightedly from one booth to another, pushing through the crowds to gawk at the variety of goods for sale. There were cages of hissing geese and clucking chickens, and all manner of fresh fruits and vegetables, including plump red strawberries; luscious, ripe peaches; big, juicy tomatoes; and huge purple beets.

The princesses wandered up one crowded row and down the next, breathing in the smells of freshly baked pastries, dried herbs, and roasting chestnuts. They ran their fingers over well-crafted belts, sweet-scented candles, cloth of many colors, and beautiful leather boots.

Coming upon a booth selling shiny, red

apples, Lysandra couldn't resist a purchase. She pulled her purse from around her neck and shook out a few gold coins. "Four, please," she said.

The merchant took the coins from her hand. "Thank you, miss." He handed her the apples and Lysandra passed them out to her friends.

"Mmm," said Fatima, taking a bite. "Delicious."

"Have you ever eaten roasted chestnuts?" asked Tansy, the juice from her apple running down her chin.

"No," said Fatima. "We don't have them where I come from."

"Oh, you must taste them," said Lysandra, and Elena nodded.

While they were weaving their way through the crowd to reach a woman selling chestnuts, a ragged man barrelled right into

Lysandra, knocking her over. Without even stopping to see if she was okay, the man plowed past the girls and disappeared.

Fatima frowned. "How rude!" She and Elena helped Lysandra to her feet.

"Are you all right?" asked Tansy.

"I'm fine," said Lysandra, brushing the dirt from her cloak. But when they reached the chestnut booth and she went to draw up her purse, it wasn't there. "My purse!" she exclaimed. "It's gone!"

Jack Flack

SUDDENLY, FROM A PLACE DEEP IN THE MARKET, someone screamed. Lysandra followed the sound with her eyes. Waving his arms wildly to ward off an angry swarm of bees was the same ragged man who had knocked her down only moments before. Lysandra could guess what had happened. "Follow me!" she yelled to her friends.

The four princesses wound their way

through the crowd to where the pitiful man stood shrieking. A circle had cleared around him; no one wanted to get near the bees. Lysandra spied her open purse lying in the dust at the man's feet. The neck strap had been cut. She hadn't felt a thing when he'd taken the purse.

Darting into the circle, Lysandra grabbed her purse and shut it. Instantly the bees flew straight up into the sky and disappeared. "Thank you, miss," the man murmured sheepishly. He was covered with puffy red welts where the bees had stung him.

Lysandra frowned. "If you needed money, you could've just asked. I would've given you some."

The man bowed his head. "Sorry, miss."

Elena stepped forward. "Those stings must hurt. Let me give you something to soothe them."

The man smiled, and Lysandra could see that several of his teeth were missing. "You're very kind, miss," he said to Elena. She poured a teaspoonful of lotion from her small blue bottle into his palm. "Rub it over each sting," she directed him.

The man did, and the painful welts disappeared. He looked at Elena in surprise. "It's magic!"

Lysandra opened her purse. Taking out a few gold coins, she held them out to the man.

"For me, miss?"

Lysandra nodded.

The man's eyes misted over. "I'm ever so grateful, miss." Taking the coins, he bowed. "Name's Jack Flack," he said, pointing to himself. "If you ever need any help, just give a whistle and I'll be at your service." Bowing again, he put the coins in his pocket and sauntered off.

"He'll probably just spend the money on ale," Fatima remarked as the princesses watched him leave.

"Maybe," said Elena. "But we can't know that for sure. Doing a kindness is never wrong."

A short while later, as they continued to walk through the market, the princesses came upon a puppet show. They laughed as three billy goats on strings danced along to a wooden bridge. Under the bridge, a puppet troll was sleeping. Suddenly he jerked to life on his strings. "Who's that crossing over my bridge?" he roared.

Lysandra felt a hand on her shoulder. "Who's that sneaking out of the castle?" someone hissed in her ear. Lysandra jumped and gave a startled yelp. *Owen!* She hadn't seen him since he and his friends had begun playing by the stables. She hadn't missed him either.

Owen smiled nastily. All the princesses

were staring at him. "Aren't you going to introduce me to your friends?"

Lysandra sighed. "Fatima, Elena, and Tansy, this is my cousin Owen."

Owen looked from one girl to the other, then back to Lysandra. "My, my," he said, smirking. "I don't think your parents will be too happy to hear about this. Stealing away to the village in disguise. And during your nap

time, too! They'll probably send your new friends packing." He paused and held out his hand, palm up. "Unless . . . "

"Unless what?" growled a voice. Suddenly Owen's feet left the ground as he was hauled up by the front of his shirt. "Excuse me, miss," Jack said. "Is this gent bothering you?"

Lysandra nodded.

Owen struggled like a worm on a hook.

"Put me down! I'll have you know, my father is the Duke of Brithia."

"Is that so?" said Jack. "Then I'm sure he'll be real interested to know what you've been up to, threatening these young misses."

"They're not 'young misses,'" Owen spat out. "They're *princesses*."

Eyeing their old cloaks, Jack Flack winked at the four girls. "Of course they are," he said. "And I'm the King of Zamora." He drew Owen toward him until they were nose to nose. "These young misses are friends of mine. In the future you'll be staying away from them, understand?"

Owen nodded. His chin wobbled as he tried not to cry.

"Good," said Jack. He set Owen down. "Because if I ever hear of you bothering one of them again . . . " He drew a finger across his throat.

Without a backward glance, Owen bounded away like a frightened rabbit.

"Thank you," Lysandra said, opening her purse.

"No, miss," Jack said quickly. "It should be plain I'm no angel. You've already given me more than I deserve." Whistling, he waved good-bye and went on his way.

"Not that I'm ungrateful," Fatima said, "but I thought *we* were going to help someone—instead of the other way around."

"But isn't it good to give *and* to receive?" Elena asked.

"You're right," said Lysandra. "But maybe it's still not too late to find someone who needs our help."

Tansy's eyes twinkled. "I have an idea." She drew her flute from her pocket and began to play. As the notes flowed, a tide of thoughts swirled through the air. If the princesses hadn't concentrated so hard on hearing them, the thoughts would've been lost in the conversations of the crowd. As it was, no one but the princesses seemed to hear them.

Lysandra watched a scowling woman take a plucked chicken from a nearby butcher. The woman's thoughts drifted toward Lysandra like smoke from a fire. *I just know I'm being cheated,* she thought. *This chicken is so scrawny, it couldn't weigh more than a handful of feathers.*

Sour old woman, thought the butcher. *I give her the best I can for her few coins, but still she thinks I'm cheating her. I can see it in her face.*

Turning her head in another direction, Lysandra spotted a beautiful girl flirting with a cobbler. *He's not good enough to kiss my boots, but I shall make him want to,* she thought.

Iris is pretty, the cobbler thought, *but I'll*

take a plain girl with a good heart any day.

Lysandra turned again. *Woe is me,* came a sad voice. *No one will ever know I'm a prince.* Startled, Lysandra glanced around but couldn't locate the voice's source. Then she heard it again. *No princess will ever want to marry me*, the voice moaned. *And I've only myself to blame.*

Lysandra looked at Fatima. "Do you hear him too?" she whispered.

Fatima nodded. "A *prince*—here in the marketplace? But where?"

"Shh," said Elena. Dropping to her hands and knees in a very unprincesslike fashion, she began searching the ground near their feet as Tansy continued to play.

"What're you doing?" asked Fatima. "The prince can't be *that* short!"

Suddenly Elena lunged forward, catching

something between her hands. She scrambled to her feet. "He's not your traditional prince," she told them, opening her hands. "He's a *frog* prince."

Prince Jerome

THE PRINCESSES STARED AT THE LARGE GREEN frog in Elena's hands. He blinked at them and began to croak rapidly. Lysandra bent closer. "I think he's trying to speak," she said. "I can almost make out some words."

"The market's too noisy," said Fatima. "Let's take him someplace quieter."

"How about the meadow where we landed?" suggested Tansy.

"Good idea," said Elena.

They left the market and walked back to the meadow. Tansy played her flute along the way, and their thoughts drifted above them. Fatima reddened when she heard herself think, *I wish I could be the one to carry him. After all I am the oldest.* A moment later Lysandra blushed too. *Maybe Fatima will let me fly the carpet when we go back to the castle*, she had thought.

By the time they reached the meadow, the princesses had learned to concentrate their attention on the frog to make his thoughts soar above their own. *Who are these girls? What new misery is this*? he thought as they set him down. *I'm still a prince, even if I am a frog. Why can't I ever get any respect?*

"Be quiet, you silly frog," Lysandra said. "We're here to help you."

The frog blinked. Then, for the first time, he spoke clearly. "Really? You're going to help me?"

The princesses nodded. "We know you're an enchanted prince," said Elena. "We heard your thoughts while Tansy was playing her flute."

"My thoughts?" squeaked the frog. "You've

been spying on my thoughts?" He jumped up and down. "That's just not right," he spluttered. "Not right at all!"

Fatima rolled her eyes. "Sounds to me like he doesn't want our help," she said to her friends. "Maybe we should just chuck him in the swamp and go back to the castle."

The frog blinked again. "The castle? What castle?"

"The castle of King Sheldon II," said Lysandra. "He's my father."

For a second the frog looked puzzled. "I've heard that name before," he said. "A long time ago. Must've been important, but—wait!" he exclaimed. "You must be a princess!"

Lysandra grinned. "We're *all* princesses." One by one, they introduced themselves.

"So now that you know our names," said Elena, picking up the frog and placing him in Fatima's lap, "won't you tell us your own?"

"I'm Prince Jerome," he said. "Or at least I used to be, before a witch placed a spell on me."

"How long ago was that?" asked Lysandra.

"Nine years ago," Jerome said sadly. "Nine l-o-n-g years ago."

Tansy whistled. "What have you been doing all that time?"

"I lived with the witch for a while," said Jerome. "But then she threw me out. I've

never understood why, since I tried to be helpful. I showed her the proper way to stir potions, and gave her good suggestions for improving her wardrobe. She wore way too much black."

Fatima smiled. "I can't imagine why she didn't appreciate your help."

Jerome sighed. "Ever since the witch kicked me out of her hut, I've been roaming from one place to another. It's a miracle I'm still alive, really. You can't imagine how close I've come to being crushed by a cart wheel or swallowed up by a goose."

He hopped to Fatima's shoulder. "In all my years as a frog, you're the first princesses I've come upon." He eyed them each in turn. "So, which one of you is going to kiss me?"

Back to the Castle

Fatima shuddered in disgust. "Not me," she said hurriedly.

Lysandra shook her head. "Nor me."

"Sorry," said Elena. "I'm not even allowed to date until I'm at least fourteen."

"Me neither," said Tansy. "And I'll probably never date. If all princes are like my brothers, I don't *ever* want to get married."

Jerome scowled. "Well, someone has to do it. It's only proper. That's the way these things are *always* done!"

"You sound just like my sister," said Lysandra. She snapped her fingers. "That's it! We'll get *her* to kiss him. They'd make a perfect match!"

"Yes!" cried the others.

"Excuse me," said Jerome. "But would you mind telling me a little more about your sister first?"

"What do you want to know?" Lysandra asked.

A rosy glow spread from Jerome's head to his feet. "Well . . . um . . . is she pretty?"

Lysandra hadn't known frogs could blush. But maybe it was only the enchanted ones that could. She grinned. "My sister has classic princess good looks right down to her golden locks."

Jerome nodded, looking pleased. "And how old is she?"

"Twenty-five," Lysandra said, somewhat reluctantly.

Jerome exploded. "TWENTY-FIVE!"

"A very *young* twenty-five," Lysandra insisted.

Fatima raised an eyebrow. "Pardon me," she said to Jerome, "but how old are *you*?"

"Let me think," said Jerome. "I've been a frog for nine years, and I was a prince up until the age of eighteen, so that would make me . . . "

"TWENTY-SEVEN!" shouted Tansy.

The princesses laughed. "You're not so young yourself," said Lysandra. "You weren't married before that witch cast a spell on you, were you?"

Jerome shook his head no. "You'll probably find this hard to believe, but I used to be rather fussy. There were lots of princesses interested in marrying me, but I rejected them all."

"Why?" Elena asked.

Jerome stared down at his webbed toes as if he felt ashamed. "Oh, I had lots of reasons. One of them laughed too loudly. Another's hair was too curly." He paused. "There was one whom I almost married. She was a real beauty, and we got along wonderfully well. We

were even engaged. . . ." His voice drifted off.

"So what happened?" asked Fatima.

"One night during dinner, she got a little piece of boiled cabbage stuck between her teeth. I couldn't help noticing. I guess I made a face, because suddenly she jumped up from the table and ran out of the room."

"And you didn't run after her?" asked Tansy.

"No," Jerome answered sadly. "I still would've married her, but she disappeared

that very night. The next day I went searching for her—and that's when I ran into the witch."

"Bad luck," said Lysandra.

"That's what I thought too," said Jerome. "But later the witch told me she'd turned me into a frog to teach me a lesson."

"And what lesson was that?" Elena asked.

"I'm not sure," said Jerome, "but she called me a perfectly proper, pathetically pompous pest when she threw me out of her hut." He sighed. "I've changed, though. Really I have."

The princesses exchanged a smile.

From far above the village, trumpets sounded. Lysandra went pale. "The rest period is over!" she exclaimed. "If we're not back in my bedchamber soon, we're doomed!"

"Then let's go!" cried Tansy.

"We'll hurry," Elena said.

Fatima scooped up Jerome in one hand

and unstrapped the carpet from her back with the other. The carpet fell to the ground and unrolled. As soon as they'd scrambled onto it, they were lifted into the air.

"Frogs don't fly!" Jerome screamed, hopping up and down in Fatima's hands.

Elena and Tansy couldn't help giggling.

"Be brave," Fatima said. "You're a *prince*, remember?" She turned to Lysandra. "Since I've got my hands full, do you want to try to fly?"

"But I don't know how," Lysandra replied.

"Don't worry," said Fatima. "It's easy. Just take hold of the front of the carpet and tug gently in the direction you want to fly. Pull up to rise and down to lower. And let go when you want to stop."

"All right." Grasping the front edge of the carpet, Lysandra pulled up. The carpet whooshed into the sky. When it looked as if they were level with the castle, Lysandra pulled forward. The carpet shot straight ahead.

As they sped along, Jerome yelped, "Put me back on the ground! I don't like it up here! We're all going to be killed! I've changed my mind! I'd rather be a live frog than a dead prince!"

Fatima rolled her eyes. "Oh, do be quiet!"

When they reached the castle, Lysandra aimed the carpet right for her bedchamber window. They sailed through it quite easily. Then Lysandra dropped the edge of the carpet, and they jerked to an abrupt halt.

"Sorry," she said as everyone tumbled to the floor.

Jerome flew out of Fatima's hands and landed with a *plop* in the middle of Gabriella's bed. With a loud "CROAK!" he hid under her pillow.

The princesses picked themselves up. "You

did really well," said Fatima. "Landings are hard. I've been flying for years, and I still muff some of mine."

Running footsteps sounded in the corridor outside the door. "Pretend we just woke up," Lysandra whispered, jumping into her bed.

A moment later Gabriella rushed into the room. "Thank goodness you're here!" she exclaimed. She fanned herself with her hands. "I had such a fright just now. I had a dream that I looked out the window and saw the four of you sailing by on a flying carpet and . . . " She stopped, her eyes narrowing as she spied the carpet in a heap on the floor. "You weren't flying just now, were you?"

With a loud croak, Jerome hopped out from under Gabriella's pillow. She screamed. "What's that *creature* doing on my bed!"

Jerome blinked, then sat still, as if stunned.

Tansy made a grab for him, but Jerome

came to and hopped out of her reach onto a pedestal table. "It's just a frog," she said. "I found him in the courtyard."

Gabriella frowned. "Please get him out of our room. Put him back outside."

"Maybe he's enchanted," Lysandra said slyly. "I think I'll kiss him and find out."

Gabriella peered at Jerome. "Don't be ridiculous. Anyone can see he's just a plain, ordinary frog." She touched his head. "He's dirty, too. Who knows what kind of awful swamp he was mucking about in before he came here."

Lysandra rather expected Jerome to speak up and defend himself, but he seemed to have lost his tongue.

"Pardon me," said Elena. "But doesn't it say in *Courtly Manners and Duties* that if a frog enters a princess's chamber, it's her duty to kiss him in case he's a prince?"

Gabriella looked at her sharply. "There may be something like that, but . . . "

"I'd kiss him myself," said Elena. "But on page forty-three, I believe it says the princess must be fifteen or older."

"Bats and bullfrogs!" Fatima exclaimed, pretending to be disappointed. "I won't be fifteen for nearly three more years!"

"And I'm only nine," Tansy said sadly. "Is *anyone* here fifteen or older?" she asked, looking innocently at Gabriella.

Gabriella blushed. "I am, but—"

"You're *way* older than fifteen," Lysandra interrupted. She knew Gabriella hated to be reminded of her age. "I bet you're even too old for frogs." She turned to Elena. "Does *Courtly Manners and Duties* give a *maximum* age for princesses who kiss frogs?"

"I don't remember," said Elena. "Shall I look it up?"

Gabriella glared at them. "I am *not* too old to kiss a frog." To prove it, she bent over Jerome, her upper lip curled in distaste. Then, closing her eyes, she planted a kiss on his little froggy mouth.

The Reunion

POOF! A HUGE PUFF OF SMOKE APPEARED AND, within moments, Prince Jerome had regained his princely shape. The girls all stared at the handsome prince perched on Gabriella's pedestal table.

"Jerome?" Gabriella asked. "Is that you?"

"Gabby!" he yelled.

Lysandra's mouth dropped open. *Gabby?*

"I knew it was you as soon as I saw you,"

said Jerome. He took Gabriella's hand in his. "You haven't changed a bit, and you're still as beautiful as ever."

Gabriella blushed. "I always wondered what happened to you," she said. "I couldn't face you after what happened that night—that horrible piece of cabbage! After I left the table, I saw myself in the mirror, and I

knew I had to flee."

Jerome shook his head. "I shouldn't have let you go. I searched for you the next day, but that's when the witch found me."

Gabriella sighed. "For the last nine years, I haven't eaten a single forkful of boiled cabbage, and I've tried to be as perfect as possible."

"Darling," Jerome said, with more tenderness than Lysandra had imagined him capable of. "I've been a fool. No one is perfect, least of all me. But if you'll give me another chance, I'll try to make you happy."

Gabriella's face lit up. "Are you saying . . . "

"Yes," said Jerome, dropping to his knee. "Will you marry me, Princess Gabriella?"

"Yes, yes," she answered. "A thousand times yes!"

"Hooray!" shouted Lysandra and her friends.

Jerome and Gabriella grinned sheepishly. Then, in front of everyone, Jerome gave Gabriella a great big kiss on the lips.

The wedding date was set for the next week to give Jerome's parents and younger brother time to travel to Zamora. His family was overjoyed to find out that he was still alive. When they arrived, there were lots of hugs and kisses and tears as Jerome's parents greeted their long-lost son and future daughter-in-law.

As Lysandra and her friends waited to be introduced, Elena pointed to the handsome young man shaking hands with Jerome. "That must be Jerome's brother," she said.

Lysandra nodded. "Gabriella says Jonathon was only four the first time she and Jerome were engaged."

"He must be thirteen now," said Tansy.

"He's very good-looking," said Fatima in a dreamy sort of voice.

Just then, Jonathon looked up and saw the princesses. He smiled and came toward them.

Fatima blushed. "I hope he didn't hear what I just said," she whispered.

The princesses introduced themselves. Then Jonathon said, "This is a beautiful place. I'd sure like a tour."

Lysandra grinned. "I bet Fatima will take you. She's got a flying carpet. From the sky, you can see all over the grounds."

Jonathon's face lit up. "I've never been on a flying carpet before. Would you mind?" he asked Fatima.

Fatima blushed again. "I'd be happy to take you."

After Fatima and Jonathon had gone, the

princesses went up to Lysandra's room. It was over an hour before Fatima rejoined them.

"Have a good time?" Lysandra teased.

Fatima smiled. "Mm-hmm."

"Find out much about him?" Elena asked.

Fatima nodded. "He's really interested in magic. He's been studying with a wizard for a year, and already he can do small transformations."

"Like what?" asked Tansy.

"Well, after we landed, we went to the kitchen. He changed a cooking pot into an apple for me."

"How did it taste?" Lysandra asked.

Fatima made a face. "A bit like iron."

The princesses laughed. Lysandra looked forward to getting to know Jonathon better. After all, once Jerome and Gabriella were married tomorrow, she and Jonathon would almost be family.

A Sweet Ending

HUNDREDS OF PEOPLE CAME TO THE WEDDING the next afternoon—nobles and villagers alike. Lysandra had invited Jack Flack, but she'd made him promise to leave the other guests' purses alone.

It was a pleasantly sunny day. The ceremony took place on the stage that had been built for the talent show. The rosebushes were in full bloom, and garlands of white gardenias wound around the stage's pillars. Gabriella wore a gown with an embroidered silk bodice and a lacy train sparkling with diamonds. To Lysandra she looked like a beautiful white butterfly.

After the ceremony Lysandra spotted Owen in the crowd of guests. He gave her a nasty look and started to walk toward her.

"Oh, great," said Tansy. "Here comes trouble."

But before Owen could reach them, Jack Flack stepped into his path. Owen turned pale, then bolted away. Jack smiled at Lysandra and tipped his hat.

At the wedding feast Gabriella was positively glowing as she sat beside Jerome. The Royal Chef had outdone himself. The buffet table groaned under huge roasts of beef and pork, and platters of fish and vegetables. A gigantic silver bowl of fruit, as well as a great slab of cheese, stood in the center.

As Lysandra helped herself to the asparagus

in white sauce, she glanced toward Gabriella. She smiled to see the large helping of boiled cabbage on her sister's plate.

Jugglers and tumblers entertained the guests as they ate. They put on a splendid show. Balls whizzed through the air, narrowly missing the guests. And at one point, the boy at the top of a human pyramid toppled into a punch bowl.

Out of the corner of her eye, Lysandra saw Jonathon sneaking peeks at Fatima. "I think he likes you," Lysandra whispered. Fatima blushed.

When the banquet was over, the guests began to leave. Jerome's family was leaving too. Jerome and Gabriella would be going with them, but riding ahead in their own carriage.

Lysandra felt a pang of regret for all the times she'd wished her sister gone. She hugged Gabriella through the carriage window. "I'll miss you," she said.

Gabriella hugged her back. "We'll still see

each other," she promised. "I'll be back to visit three or four times a year. And we'll find a time to chat at least once a week through the Crystal Ball Room."

That night the princesses decided to have a midnight picnic and one last flying carpet ride. Sneaking down to the kitchen in their nightgowns, they packed a basket with bread and cheese, olives, custard, almonds, and cider.

As they were leaving to go back upstairs, Fatima stumbled into a bench and stubbed her toe. "Bats and bullfrogs!" she yelped, hopping around on one foot.

"Shh," said Lysandra, stifling a giggle. Fortunately, no one seemed to have heard them.

Soon the four princesses were sailing through Lysandra's window and over the castle walls. Moonlight glittered on the moat as they floated down to the village below, landing in the very same meadow they'd visited when they'd rescued Jerome.

Lysandra opened the basket and set everything on top of the carpet. The princesses dived into the food. Fatima grabbed a handful of almonds. "I can't believe I'm hungry again after eating so much at the banquet."

Elena reached for a piece of bread. "Maybe being in love gives you an appetite."

Lysandra and Tansy giggled.

"I'm *not* in love," Fatima protested. Then she smiled. "But I may be in *like*."

When the girls finished their picnic, Lysandra and Fatima lifted the carpet and shook off the crumbs.

Elena cocked her head. "I think I hear music. It's coming from somewhere in the village."

The princesses listened and began clapping their hands to the lively tune. "Let's dance!" Lysandra yelled.

"Yes, let's!" cried Tansy.

The four princesses joined hands, and Lysandra led them in a merry dance all around the meadow. If only this night could go on forever, she thought. But at last her feet grew tired. Lysandra collapsed onto the ground, taking the others with her.

Giggling, Fatima sat up. "Time for bed?" she said, stifling a yawn.

"Afraid so," said Elena.

Lysandra retrieved the basket, and the four princesses settled themselves on Fatima's carpet. Then they sailed back to the castle and tumbled into bed.

The next morning it was time for Fatima, Elena, and Tansy to return home. "I'm going to miss you so much," said Lysandra as they stood around the carriages in the courtyard. "You're the best friends a princess could ever have."

"Likewise," said Tansy.

Fatima stood with her flying carpet tucked under one arm. "I don't know when I've had such fun."

"If I had sisters," Elena said softly, "I'd want them to be just like you three."

Lysandra stared at the ground, a lump in her throat. Elena put an arm around her. "Don't worry. I'm sure we'll meet again soon."

Tansy nodded. "And if we keep our eyes and ears open, one of us is sure to discover a new adventure."

"In the meantime, we can keep in touch through our crystal balls," said Fatima.

Lysandra cheered up. "Of course we can."

Hugging one another, the princesses said good-bye. Then Tansy and Elena climbed into their carriages, and Fatima unrolled her carpet.

As the carriages clattered over the draw-bridge and Fatima rose into the sky, Lysandra thought how wonderfully everything had turned out. She hoped they all would meet again soon. With her magical purse, Tansy's flute, Elena's lotion, and Fatima's carpet, they could go anywhere and do anything. They had power—*princess power*! Lysandra could hardly wait for their next adventure.

AND NOW FOR A SNEAK PEEK AT

Princess Power #2:
The Charmingly Clever Cousin

Princess Fatima

PRINCESS FATIMA SHIFTED IN HER CHAIR AND glanced longingly at her flying carpet, leaning against the Royal Nursery wall. She'd give anything to be on her carpet right now, soaring over the countryside.

A soft cry drew her attention to the sleeping baby in her lap. Fatima studied her nephew's bald head. It looked like a squashed pumpkin and was much too big for his body.

Drool wetted his chin. When he was awake, all Prince Hassim did was burp, spit up, and cry. *Boring.*

Fatima wondered what her friends—the princesses Lysandra, Elena, and Tansy—were doing right now. Two months had passed since they'd first met. Two *long* months. Whatever her princess friends were up to had to be a lot more exciting than this.

Fatima sighed. She didn't really like babysitting, but she hadn't wanted to refuse when her sister, Selime, asked for her help. After all, Fatima didn't get to see Selime very often. Even by flying carpet, it took two whole days to reach the palace where her sister and brother-in-law, Prince Ahmed, lived.

Rising carefully so as not to wake him, Fatima carried Hassim to his Royal Cradle. Laying the sleeping baby down, she tiptoed away. With luck, maybe he'd nap for a couple of hours. Then she'd be free to do something fun for a change. Perhaps she could even get out of the palace for a while.

Fatima glanced at her carpet again. Would it be so wrong to take a quick flight into town and spend a few minutes wandering through the bazaar? She hadn't flown anywhere in the past two weeks. She longed to run her fingers through the colorful silk scarves and sample the candied stuffed dates the merchants sold.

But even as Fatima thought about leaving, a stern voice echoed inside her head. It was Prince Ahmed's voice, scolding her for nearly dropping baby Hassim when she had run with him down the hall last night. She'd only wanted to be in time to see the acrobats perform in the Grand Hall before dinner!

Later, when she came to Ahmed and Selime's room to apologize, she'd overheard him talking with her sister. "Fatima is much too young and irresponsible to take care of Hassim," he'd declared.

Hidden behind the door, Fatima had imagined the frown on his less-than-handsome face, with eyebrows that were too bushy and a nose that was somewhat pointed. Prince Ahmed was no Prince Charming—except, of course, to her sister.

"She's twelve," Selime had said. "That's old enough."

"For some girls, perhaps," Ahmed had replied. "But Fatima is too impulsive. She does things without considering if her actions could be dangerous. Hassim could get hurt!"

"Babies are always getting hurt," Selime had said calmly. "Why, just the other day, he grabbed at my tiara while I was holding him and scratched his little arm."

Fatima felt a rush of gratitude toward her sister for sticking up for her. Honestly! Prince Ahmed was *so* overprotective. When it came to Hassim, he was fussier than a mother hen with her chicks. Instead of apologizing, Fatima had turned on her heels and gone back to her room.

Now, a knock on the Royal Nursery door made Fatima jump. She hurried to open it. "Shh," she said to the kitchen maid standing outside. "Prince Hassim is asleep."

The kitchen maid was a skinny girl with rosy cheeks. As she lowered her eyes and curtsied, her long, dark pigtail fell over one shoulder. "Pardon me, Princess. The Royal Chef sent me to ask what you'd like for lunch."

A large helping of free time, Fatima almost said. Then an idea popped into her head. "What's your name?" she asked.

"Nar, Your Highness," the girl replied.

"How old are you, Nar?"

"Fourteen."

Fatima nodded. If *she*, at twelve, was old enough to watch a baby, surely a girl of fourteen was even better. Besides, it would only be for a short while. . . .

Find out what happens to Fatima and her friends in the next Princess Power adventure!